NIGHTSHADE

USA TODAY BESTSELLER

JEN TALTY

NIGHTSHADE

A Family Affair Novella, Book One

JEN TALTY

USA Today Bestselling Author

"I positively loved *In Two Weeks*, and highly recommend it. The writing is wonderful, the story is fantastic, and the characters will keep you coming back for more. I can't wait to get my hands on future installments of the NYS Troopers series." *Long and Short Reviews*

"*In Two Weeks* hooks the reader from page one. This is a fast paced story where the development of the romance grabs you emotionally and the suspense keeps you sitting on the edge of your chair. Great characters, great writing, and a believable plot that can be a warning to all of us." *Desiree Holt, USA Today Bestseller*

"*Dark Water* delivers an engaging portrait of wounded hearts as the memorable characters take you on a healing journey of love. A mysterious death brings danger and intrigue into the drama, while sultry passions brew into a believable plot that melts the reader's heart. Jen Talty pens an entertaining romance that grips the heart as the colorful and dangerous story unfolds into a chilling ending." *Night Owl Reviews*

"This is not the typical love story, nor is it the typical mystery. The characters are well rounded and interesting." *You Gotta Read Reviews*

"Deadly Secrets is the best of romance and suspense in one hot read!" *NYT Bestselling Author Jennifer Probst*

"A charming setting and a steamy couple heat up the pages in an suspenseful story I couldn't put down!" *NY Times and USA today Bestselling Author Donna Grant*

"Murder in Paradise Bay is a fast-paced romantic thriller with plenty of twists and turns to keep you guessing until the end. You won't want to miss this one..." *USA Today bestselling author Janice Maynard*

PROLOGUE

*ne month ago…*
Bronx, NY

California Banister, or Cali as everyone called her, pressed her hands firmly on the tabletop as she sucked in a deep breath. One half of her wanted to reach across the table and squeeze the life out of the sleazeball sitting across from her.

The other half wanted to lecture her parents on reading the fine print, only she knew the asshole who'd talked them into this partnership had made sure they buried the clause, using complicated legal speak so deep into the contract that it would most likely take a seasoned attorney to find it and recommend her parents not sign it. Of course, that would mean they were given the time to consult someone…anyone. However, Mr. Thompson, the mob's muscle disguised as a kind businessman, put the fear of God in her parents.

"I think I'm being very generous in my offer," Mr.

Thompson, the sleazeball, said with a condescending smile that made Cali wish she didn't understand the penalty for premeditated murder.

"I want it in writing," she said, holding her ground.

Thompson frowned.

She cleared her throat. "A simple contract that I'll have my attorney draw up that will null and void my parents' current contract if I pay you two hundred and fifty thousand by the end of the year." That gave her eleven months to sell her soul to the devil. But she'd do anything to make sure her parents didn't lose their family restaurant to some jerk-off who gave them a loan, knowing the stipulation that if they went under a certain earning level, he'd be able to buy them out for pennies, essentially kicking them out of their own business with very little to show for it.

"Why don't you let us draw up the contract?" Thompson cocked his head, giving her a kind smile. The man sure did know how to turn on the charm. "We don't want to worry your pretty little—"

"I'll have the paperwork sent over to your office by morning." They had no idea she'd be drafting the document herself. Even though she was kissing a career as a lawyer down the tubes before she even set foot in law school, making sure her parents kept their business would be well worth it.

"Mr. Carlucci was hoping we'd have all this cleared up today," Thompson said.

"One more day isn't going to harm your boss much." Cali had a four-year degree in political science, though it took her six years to get, and she figured in one year, after her contract as an employee of Nightshade Corporation, she'd be able to find a decent job, if she wasn't arrested for prostitution first.

She swallowed the thick lump that formed in her throat. If her parents knew her role at Nightshade as a *companion*, they'd fall dead of heartache and shame. However, the twenty thousand a month living expenses to keep wealthy men company took the sting out.

But not the bile that sloshed about her gut like a category five hurricane. She reminded herself that these men would buy her gifts that she could sell and give her cash she could pocket. She figured she'd have the money with a day or two to spare.

She just hoped she got some old man who just wanted a pretty face, and sex wouldn't be part of the equation. Or if the latter was required, she only hoped she could live with herself afterward.

"If you don't get us the money by December thirty-first, everything gets turned over to Mr. Carlucci."

"But if I get it to you, my parents buy the restaurant back for the price of one dollar."

Talk about a gamble. Right now, her parents could walk away with twenty-five grand, which was a shitty-ass deal to begin with, but better than if she failed.

Failure was not an option.

One month ago…
  Scarsdale, NY

William Xavier Sumner III, better known as Xavier, paced in the hallway outside of his father's home office. It had been three years since he'd sat on the other side of the old man's desk while his father chopped up his credit cards and depleted his trust fund all in the name of forcing Xavier to show the old man he had what it took to be successful as an investigative journalist, versus joining the family business. At twenty-four, he'd landed a book agent and had his first proposal in a bidding war with three different well-known publishers, getting him a hefty first advance.

At twenty-five, his first book hit the NY Times list, which had been the icing on the cake.

He'd achieved most of the goals he'd set out in his four-year plan, a year early.

Now he was sitting on potentially the largest story about organized crime and its connection to the Nightshade Corporation, which Xavier had on good authority, ran a high-end men's club. He choked on the thought. No matter how you dressed it up, Nightshade ran a prostitution ring. All Xavier needed to do was prove that the women employed were with their assigned men under duress.

And that they were paid for sex.

But he needed his father's help.

And his money.

The heavy, mahogany door pushed open into the hallway. His father waved him in. His mother and youngest sister, Finley, now a freshman in college, double majoring in finance and economics, sat on the sofa to the right of the desk, leaving Xavier to sit in the wing-back across from the desk.

His little sister had her long, strawberry-blond hair pulled into a bun at the nape of her neck. Her dark-rimmed glasses, which made her look much older, were perched on her nose while she scanned a document. His mother sat with her legs crossed at the ankle and smiled. Her brown hair was cut short to her chin and while she had a few wrinkles around the eyes, she didn't look a day over forty, making her look more like Finley's sister instead of her mother.

Xavier took his seat and awaited his fate.

"Interesting proposal," his father said, rocking back in his oversized chair. "I'm no longer surprised why you had us sign a non-disclosure agreement before sharing it with us."

"This could be the biggest story of my career. My sources tell me that many of the women who are employed as escorts are doing so only because they owe Carlucci and his band of cronies money. Even when they pay off their debts, they are held in strict contracts with the men who basically buy them."

"Have you seen the contracts?" his father asked. "What is the term agreement?"

"I've only seen parts of them, but it starts at a year. Sex is not stipulated, but the document clearly states that it's allowed if both parties are agreeable. However, my source tells me it's expected, and those that don't do as they are told, well, some go missing, some end up dead, and some end up beaten into submission. One woman I interviewed said she was allowed out of her contract after she called the police, but only if she signed a two-year contract with a different gentleman. Because her family owed a shit ton of money to the mob, she did it." Xavier revisited the urge to stand and pace. Something he did often while talking through a story. Instead, he snapped his fingers, cracking his knuckles and ignoring his mother's glare.

"Is this woman your source?" his father asked with an arched brow and a tickle of a smile.

"She's stopped all communication with me since signing that new contract. All I can tell you about my source is they work inside Nightshade. I'm confident if you help me with this, I can bring down the biggest prostitution and human-trafficking ring this state has ever seen."

"Messing with the mafia is a dangerous game," his little

5

sister said as if she'd had any real-world experience with them, which she hadn't. But she did understand the game of chance; statistically speaking, he was playing in a high-stakes game of poker.

"Leaving it alone, knowing what I know, would be turning my back on a major crime. I can't do that," Xavier said with a tight tone. Knowing that Susan Carl had agreed to be shifted to another rich man to be used, or sold to some whacko overseas, made his blood boil. Susan hadn't been any older than twenty-two and behind her badly beaten face, he had seen a pretty young woman who had her innocence stripped. What happened to her would change who she was forever, and Xavier didn't want that to happen to anyone else.

"Is that the only reason you're doing it?"

"That's the driving force, but all know this is the kind of story that publishers would pay a million as an advance," Xavier said, trying to hide the anxiety coating his words like a thick layer of fog. "And win me some major publishing and journalism awards."

"It could destroy your career, and you as well," his little sister said, peeking over her glasses. "Not to mention cause you bodily harm. I go to school with Trish Leonardi."

"Who is she?" his mother asked.

"Her mother is cousins with Carlucci. Trish always said she had no ties to the mob, but based on the some of the stories she told us about shakedowns and the removal of fingers as a warning, we figured she had some intimate working knowledge of Carlucci's organization."

"I hope you are exaggerating," his mother said, slack-jawed, staring at her youngest child.

"She is," Xavier said, giving his sister a sideways glance. Finley might be super book-smart and great with numbers, but she didn't have the best read on people.

And she had no filter, something she'd have to work on if she was going to take over the family business.

"It's not the days of leaving horse heads under sheets. More money laundering and not dumping bodies in the Hudson," Xavier said.

"Mom watches too much television," his father said with a nod and a bit of a scowl.

The Carluccis weren't the kind of gangsters movies were made out of, but they weren't to be taken lightly either.

"I know I'm asking for a lot, but if this works, I'll be able to pay it back in spades," Xavier said, sitting on his hands to keep them from shaking. This was worse than when he'd put a small dent in the driver door on the Lamborghini the one and only time he took it out without his father's permission.

"I'm not worried about the money," his father said, staring at the ceiling. "I've watched your career, and I have to say I'm more than impressed. You're really good at what you do."

"As if you had any doubt," his mother chimed in with a smile and a wave of her hand. "You told me the day he turned you down—"

"Dear, let's stick with the current situation."

His father's approval meant the world to Xavier. He'd hated disappointing the old man, so knowing his choice of careers left his father with a sense of pride eased the tension in Xavier's muscles.

"Do you really think this story is that big?" his father asked. "Worthy of taking such a huge risk? You're only twenty-five. Your career has barely begun." The way his father narrowed his eyes, Xavier knew he understood the potential for bodily harm but didn't want to say anything in front of Xavier's mother, something Xavier appreciated.

"Best case scenario is I blow the Carluccis and Nightshade out of the water. That will land me more than a big fat advance. The potential for a television documentary would be huge and something I'd love to be involved in. The worst case is I move on to another story," he said. Only there was no way in hell he'd move on. This was a once in a lifetime opportunity, and Xavier was taking the bull by the horns.

His father tried to conceal a smile by running his hand over his mouth, his thumb and forefinger gliding over the corners. "You can use the house in Montauk. It will be freezing, since it's winter, but I'll have the staff turn everything on. I also want your word that you will leave the security cameras on."

"Not inside the house, I won't," Xavier answered a little too quickly. "Oh my," his mother mumbled. "I hadn't thought about what might be—"

"Mom," Xavier said with heat rushing to his cheeks. "I don't plan on taking advantage of the young lady. You raised me better than that, but I can't be worried about you all checking in on me. That's just too weird."

"You can turn the monitoring off, but I'd feel better if you kept them running internally. You can check them in my office. That way you can see what she might be up to, or if she has any of the other employees over. We do have a fair amount of valuables."

"I don't like the sound of this," his mother said, shaking her head.

"I'll be safe." Xavier glanced at his mother with a reassuring smile. "First sign of trouble, I'll hit the panic button." Now it was time to ask one more favor that might not go over very well. "I'm hoping this doesn't take but a month." He left out that once he selected a female to be his companion, the contract was for a year, but he'd deal with that once the story broke. "But I really need to play the part, if you know what I mean."

His father held out his hand. "You can use the private jet. I'll set you up with a credit card, but I will expect you to pay that back."

"I really appreciate that, Dad. I intend on paying you back every penny. The key is to make it look like I've got millions."

"That's the easy part," his sister said. "The hard part will be if you can pull off the lifestyle anymore."

He waggled his finger at his little sister. "A little humility goes a long way."

His father laughed. "It's so nice to hear my children repeat my own words."

 *resent day…*

"WELCOME TO THE VIP LOUNGE, MR. SUMNER," Rick Oppenheim said. "We are so excited to have someone of your stature joining us."

"I'm looking forward to finding the perfect lady. My life has been so hectic since my first book came out that I don't have five minutes to even swipe left or right or whatever that is on those stupid dating apps."

Rick slapped Xavier on the shoulder. "Not to mention we do all the screening for you." Rick pushed open a set of double doors that led from the main lounge to a private room.

The stench of cigar smoke filled his throat and lungs. All of his frat buddies, as well as his friends from the country club, would occasionally light up a nice Cuban cigar. But Xavier could never tolerate them. He covered his mouth, breathing slowly, trying not to gag and cough. That wouldn't be too smooth.

"What can I get you to drink?" Rick asked.

"Scotch neat, please." His father's drink, but it seemed fitting. A beer probably wouldn't have gone over well based on all the men in the room, swirling their whiskey glasses.

"Have a seat in that back booth over there."

Casually stuffing his hands into his pockets, he made his way across the lounge. He smiled and nodded at the group of men sitting in wing-back chairs around a small table in the center. Xavier recognized one of the men as Larry Thompson, a so-called businessman who gave loans to those in need, only to rip them off in the end.

Xavier couldn't prove it. Yet. But he would. It was only a matter of time.

Rick returned with two drinks. "This part of the lounge is men only. You are welcome to use it anytime. The bar will keep a running tab, and each month you will get a bill. If you don't use it, you will be charged a seventy-five dollar service fee."

Xavier raised the whiskey glass to his lips and let the dark liquid flow down his throat. The scotch didn't burn, but he was glad he hadn't taken a larger gulp.

"Good, right?" Rick held up his glass. "Nothing like a good bottle of Bunnahabhain."

"One of my favorites." His dad's, actually, but what did it matter? "So, if women aren't allowed back here, how am I supposed to pick who I want as my companion?"

"The VIP lounge really doesn't have anything to do with Nightshade, other than all the members here have at one point used our services." Rick snapped his fingers, and one of the waiters came rushing over carrying a tablet. "We take pride in matching our clients with the perfect companion. That's why it sometimes takes a few weeks.

Between vetting new girls and making sure ones who are coming off contracts have had enough downtime—"

"Downtime?" Thus far, Xavier couldn't find a single illegal activity. Shady maybe, but nothing that could get anyone arrested.

"Many of our employees sign on for a second year with a new client, if we can match them, but we want to make sure they've been out of the limelight long enough that people like you don't start reporting on things that just aren't true." Rick raised his glass.

Xavier leaned back, tossing his free hand on the back of the booth. "You wouldn't have accepted my application if you believed my job was going to interfere with your business model."

"Only partly true." Rick pushed his glass to the side and set up the tablet on the table. "We don't like calling Nightshade an escort service because that always gives the wrong impression, but as I pointed out in your contract, there is nothing keeping you from writing any article about what we do. However, your contract with our employee will differ. Most of our women don't want to be called out." He tapped the screen, pulling up two of images of young women. "I've got three groupings. These ladies have very strict rules. They don't stay at your house, or overnight. How often they go out with you is limited."

He downed the rest of his drink as he stared into the dull eyes of women who he didn't believe had control of anything, much less calling the shots with a client. He wished he could track down all these women and help them right now. "I want someone living in my house."

Rick nodded. "I totally understand, but please remember, under no circumstance are our employees expected to have sexual relations. We aren't that kind of service."

"But it does happen, correct?"

Rick swiped the tablet screen, pausing with his hand hovering over the next two images. "What you and our employee do as consenting adults is between you. That said, she is not required. It's not at all part of the contract."

Point made.

"You mentioned the length of the contract is negotiable."

"We have a one-month trial period. If after that time, things aren't going as expected, or you're not a good match, either party can terminate, but all contracts are twelve months."

"I want the option to extend the companionship," Xavier said.

"We generally revisit that at the nine-month mark, but it's always a possibility. We have a couple of gentleman who have been with the same girl for many years. Hell, we even have two couples who ended the agreement and got married."

"Whoa. That is exactly what I'm not looking for." Not a lie. Xavier didn't have time for relationships, and he honestly hadn't had one since college. A few friends with benefits, but that's about it.

Rick laughed. "No worries. Now, for employees looking for a long-term gig, these are the two best matches to your profile." He handed Xavier a set of headphones. "I'll let you get acquainted with these two amazing women. If neither one of them tickles your fancy, we will keep searching."

One of the women had boy-short blonde hair. Hollow cheekbones, like a skinny runway model. Her eyes were a smoky gray and while she was most definitely hot, she wasn't the kind of woman anyone could believe Xavier would be interested in. Didn't matter that all of this was fake, one night in the spotlight and everyone would be speculating, and not how he had planned. He'd spent the last few weeks hinting that he'd been seeing a special lady, and he needed one to fit the bill.

He ran his fingers across the screen and sucked in a deep breath. He blinked. And swallowed.

Then did it again.

"She's perfect," he whispered, staring at the quintessential girl next door. She had long, dark hair and a sweet smile that told him she was not only smart but held a softness that couldn't be faked. Strong and independent, but not overly aggressive.

Sweet.

And her blue-green eyes expressed a kindness that melted his heart.

"California Banister." He let her name roll off his lips like honey clinging to the hive. "I want her."

Having five grand instantly pop into Cali's bank account hadn't even put a dent into what she needed to help her parents and did nothing but frazzle her nerves. However, getting the phone call that she'd been matched to a client and having another twenty grand magically appear, giving her nearly thirty-five thousand in savings, total, gave her hope.

An entire month had ticked by since she'd found out her parents were being strong-armed by Mr. Larry Thompson, who worked for a known crime family, the Carluccis, leaving her now with ten months to meet their financial demands, or her parents would lose everything.

She tugged her large rolling suitcase across the train station in Montauk and parked herself near the front door.

Every time someone stepped in or out, a burst of freezing air managed to slip inside her down jacket, prickling her skin. Wet snow fell from the dark sky. She shivered, hugging herself, waiting for Xavier Sumner to saunter into the building. The agreement she'd signed to be his companion for the next year had been simple and straightforward.

And sex wasn't part of the deal.

Though she knew that part was an unspoken contract. Every girl she'd talked to inside the organization said it eventually came with the territory.

Well, at least Xavier was eye candy.

Maybe in a couple of years she'd be able to wash off all the shame and guilt that had already started to build under her skin.

She had agreed to live in his house in Montauk, mostly because it meant more money and it was only a three-and-a-half-hour train ride back to the Bronx where she could see her family. Better than being paired with someone across the country. She further consented to attending fundraisers, parties, public appearances, among other things when needed. In essence, she was to appear to be Xavier's girlfriend for the next year.

Maybe in the summer, when it was warmer, she'd feel better about the situation. Right now, the concept chilled her bones like the white stuff blanketing the ground.

During the phone call she'd had with Xavier yesterday, he'd made it clear she'd have a bedroom suite all to herself, that sex was not a requirement, ever, but when they traveled, for the sake of appearances, they would need to share a hotel room, though he mentioned he'd do his best to always book suites or penthouses with more than one bedroom.

Must be nice to have enough money that could feed an entire country, but instead you spend it on hotel rooms.

She shoved her hands in her pockets, staring out the door, searching for the handsome face she'd seen the other day when she'd Googled him and watched a few of his crime pieces on some investigative program. At least he was young and handsome and not some fifty-year-old that wanted a pretty little thing to show off. Not that it would matter. This was strictly a business arrangement. She was providing a service and getting paid to do so.

God, that sounded like a high-class call girl if she ever heard of one.

The scene where Richard Gere picks up Julia Roberts in a car he can't drive in the movie *Pretty Woman* appeared in her brain.

No sex required, she reminded herself.

Ha! She knew it would be part of the equation eventually.

A black Range Rover with large tires rolled to a stop in front of the station. The driver's side door swung open and out stepped Xavier.

Her breath hitched as she clutched the buttons on her coat. He wore dark sunglasses, his light-brown hair buzzed close to his head. His jeans hung low on his hips. His tan work-type boots sloshed in the snow while the wind caught his unzipped North Face jacket.

How he wasn't an ice cube, she had no idea.

"Hey, Cali, sorry I'm late," he said, leaning in and kissing her cheek, letting his lips linger as if they'd known each other for more than three seconds.

"I've only been waiting for a few minutes." She eyed him while he snagged her suitcase and opened the door. She anticipated their first few minutes together to be awkward, but this was just weird until she stepped out into the cold ocean air and was nearly blinded by what she had thought was sun glare but turned out to be a man pointing a camera in their direction, shouting questions. She couldn't put the words together as she ducked into the SUV.

Xavier slammed the car into drive and sped off.

"What was that all about?" she asked.

"I made the mistake of mentioning a girlfriend in a local café where that reporter had been having coffee, watching me, wondering why I'd moved into my parents' summer home."

"I thought you owned it?" Her voice screeched worse than fingers on a chalkboard.

Xavier was only twenty-five, and he'd made his name as a reporter and now a novelist. However, he was still the son to the billionaire William Xavier Sumner II, so she assumed he had a house. Or two.

On the train, she'd read a few social media posts, bashing his book deal, saying he bought himself into publishing. Based on the work she'd seen on his television show, and his in-depth knowledge of the subject matter he reported on, she'd bet the negative attention had more to do with jealousy or sour grapes.

But what did she know?

"I own a loft in Manhattan's Upper East Side, but I needed some quiet to finish my second book, so my parents told me to use their summer place. I'm thinking I want to buy out here sometime."

Such troubles to have. "It's miserable here in the winter."

"Everywhere in New York is unbearable when it's cold." He glanced in her direction before checking out the rearview mirror. "It's nice to meet you, Cali."

She let out a slight laugh, which was cut short when she

looked over her shoulder and noticed the car the reporter had been driving was hot on their heels. Being chased by the paparazzi was the last thing she needed.

"Do they always chase you down like this?"

"No. Not usually. But don't worry. This story will die down quickly. No one cares that much about my love life or my book deal. That guy has had it in for me since I was picked for the same internship he'd applied for when we were back in high school. Let's just say he's been a bit of a stalker ever since, but harmless. And no one buys into his stories much anyway."

She pulled out her phone and brought up the social media post. "Is his name Jeff Marlin?"

"How did you know that?"

"He's been bashing you on social media." She held up her phone as they approached a stoplight heading to the north shore of Montauk facing Block Island Sound near Fort Pond Bay.

Xavier peered over his sunglasses, showing off his light-emerald eyes. He had a boyish face with his high cheekbones and rounded chin with not a speck of facial hair that she could detect. Clean cut and wholesome would be the only way to describe Xavier.

In his profile picture, he wore a golf shirt, showing off his muscular shoulders and arms. Tall and lean and sexy as hell.

"Is he getting a lot of hits or views?"

"In the thousands," she said, knowing in the scheme of things that meant Jeff didn't have a large following and that most likely anyone who came across the information had probably Googled Xavier like she had.

"Doing your research on me?" He winked, then shoved his glasses back up on his face. The Range Rover jerked forward through the green light.

"Just curious about who I'd be spending the next year with." She stared through the window, checking out all the expensive houses ranging from small two-bedroom cottages to ten-thousand-square-foot homes overlooking the beach. She'd spent two summers working at a resort in the Hamptons and as of this moment, she much preferred the look and feel of Montauk. Not that after this year she'd be returning to the area. Every penny she earned would be saved and then spent on December 31.

Actually, she hoped before that date simply because she didn't want her parents worrying anymore.

She hated lying to them about why she chose to take a year off between her four-year degree and law school, but she couldn't tell them she'd become an employee of Nightshade Corporation. Instead, she'd informed her parents she'd been offered a job working with the Sumners, specifically Xavier, helping him with the research of his new crime novel, which involved a law firm.

She had no idea what his second book would be about, but she'd deal with that later. Hopefully, they didn't go looking for information and stuck with their routine of watching only game shows on television and reading the local paper.

"Mind if I ask you a couple of questions?" He turned left onto Soundview Drive and made a quick right into a driveway. The houses in this section had to go for at least fifteen million or more. Butterflies filled her stomach.

She'd hit pay dirt.

"Go right ahead," she said with a breathy lightness similar to a spring breeze rolling in off the ocean.

"If you want to be a lawyer, why aren't you going to school right now?"

"I'm taking some time off to study for my LSATs as

well saving some money. Law school is expensive, and I don't want massive loans." Not too far from the truth.

"Makes sense." He pulled the SUV into the four-car-deep garage under the pool, a concept she'd never seen before. A car with a cover draped over it had been parked in front of the Range Rover and next to that was some kind of large motorcycle, also under a cloth cover. Rich people were so weird.

She followed him up a short staircase and into a large family room with two matching light-greenish-gray leather sofas and two white leather recliners. The floor looked like a whitewashed hardwood but felt soft under her shoes. The room had a very modern flare with a beachy feel, and it faced the ocean. The front of the house had sliding glass doors everywhere. "This is beautiful."

"Thanks," he said, setting the suitcase at the bottom of the staircase. "I'll take that up to your room after we have a cocktail and some dinner."

She nodded, letting her fingers trace the white circular dining room table, the sun beating through the clear glass, warming her face. Shedding her coat, she made her way to the breakfast bar off the kitchen. Every appliance was stainless steel and looked brand new.

"So, tell me, Cali, are you also looking for a long-term relationship past our agreement?"

She swallowed. Not a question she thought too much about. "Why don't you ask me that in about six months."

He laughed as he opened a wine cooler and pulled out two bottles. "Red or white?"

"What's for dinner?"

"Filet Mignon, sour cream and chive mashed potatoes, and asparagus. Or if you don't like that—"

"That's perfect; let's open the red."

"Works for me." He pulled out some fancy corkscrew

21

and popped open the bottle, pouring the dark-red liquid into a carafe. While she liked wine, having a bottle that cost more than ten dollars and really needed to breathe before drinking was so far out of her wheelhouse. Hell, this house was out of her league.

"I'm curious, why does a man like you go to Nightshade Corporation for companionship? I suspect you could have any woman you wanted."

Pulling down two large wine glasses, he shook his head. "This is going to sound so conceited, but that's the reason right there, and not because I think I'm all that special, but the last two women I dated were either after my family's money or thought dating me would be glamorous and give them their fifteen minutes of fame, only they figured out really quick, I'm not famous and other than the asshole who snapped our picture at the Amtrak station, no one cares what I do."

"According to our agreement, part of my role will be to attend parties and other functions."

He nodded, leaning his hip against the counter. "I do have a couple of book things I need to attend, and my parents have different events they want me at. To be totally honest, my parents think we met a few months ago. This is my way of getting them off my back, but also, I wouldn't mind settling down."

"At twenty-six?"

"You're three years younger than me and yet here you are in a year-long agreement to be my companion. Or are you in it just for the money?"

"Perhaps a little of both," she said, pressing her hands against her lap as she sat on one of the bar stools. She was only here for the money. Once this was over, she figured he'd want to terminate the arrangement, and when she'd been given her severance package, they'd go their separate ways, no harm no foul. "But, of course, I'm looking for something long-term; I just don't view it as settling down. I'm far from marriage, kids, all that. I want to finish my law degree, get a job, and then maybe settling down will be in the end game."

"What kind of lawyer do you want to be?" He poured the wine and pushed a glass in her direction.

"Criminal," she said, realizing the irony of what he did for a living.

He arched a brow and the corner of his mouth tipped upward. "Here's to the start of something potentially very interesting."

wo weeks later…

Xavier closed his laptop, satisfied with the notes he'd made so far, but not thrilled with the lack of direction or information he'd been able to gather on Larry Thompson and his connection to the Carlucci mob family and Cali and her parents' restaurant. He didn't like to make assumptions about anything, but he suspected the family business was used for money laundering. The question was how much did Mr. and Mrs. Banister know about their business dealings with Thompson.

And did Cali know anything.

More importantly, had those business dealings led to her being strong-armed into being a high-priced call girl, or had she gone into it willingly?

Pulling up the security recordings, he hit the fast forward button. He leaned back in his father's leather chair. As a kid, he used to sit in this very office, on the floor, playing with his Legos, thinking about the day he'd be able to fill out the chair. It had never been about working for his dad, just being like the man he admired most.

The only thing the security camera showed had been Cali padding down the stairs for some coffee at seven in the morning. He reached over and shut the system down, disappointment filling his mind. If she'd been lurking about at night, he'd have something to confront her with and open the can of worms that would hopefully lead to her giving him the story of the century.

His source at the VIP lounge hadn't any information at all on Cali. Honestly, his source hadn't given him much except for Susan's name. Her story catapulted Xavier into this cockamamie plan.

He stepped from his father's office and made his way toward the family room. Standing in the foyer, he leaned against the wall and stared at Cali. Snow floated gently from the sky, landing on the sandy shore. The waves crashed into the beach, pulling the snow into the frigid ocean. Once, when he was maybe six, and they'd all come out here for some Christmas party, he built a snowman on the beach, not understanding the sea would steal it. He'd pressed his hands and face against the glass, screaming before falling to the floor and tossing the best temper tantrum he could muster.

Never brought the snowman back, but the next morning, he woke up to a ten-foot one next to the pool. His dad swore he didn't make it.

Cali rolled her neck, pulling him back to the here and now. She wore his sweat pants, which he wondered where she'd gotten them from, and a long-sleeve, plain-white shirt. Her long, auburn hair curled over her shoulders while she bit down on the end of a pencil. A legal pad was in one hand, and the other held a very large paperback book that reminded him of those study guides he had to use when studying for his ACT and SAT tests.

Cali had been something unexpected. Smart, beautiful, fun to talk to, and down-to-earth. He didn't feel he had to wine and dine her, though he did enjoy cooking with her. Every night since she'd arrived, they cooked a fine meal and drank wine and got to know one another, only he was living a lie.

"You're staring at me," she said, not turning her head.

"Of course I am. You're the prettiest thing in the room." He pushed himself from the wall and made his way to the sofa, lifting her feet and setting them down on his lap.

A bold move considering they hadn't even shared a kiss.

They had a few long stares. The occasional accidental touch while cooking. But nothing overtly sensual in any way. Of course, he had been avoiding her during the day, hiding in his office, working.

More like making sure he wasn't distracted by her presence, though she'd been worming her way into his mind every second of the day.

And into his dreams at night.

None of which had anything to do with his story.

"I've never understood toe polish other than it's sexy." He brushed the tip of his forefinger over her big toe. "But in the winter, is it necessary?"

"I have a little more time on my hands than I'm used to, so." She shrugged. She acted casual around him, but there was an underlying tension seeping from her pores that he couldn't put a finger on. He'd grown up being used to women treating him like an object. Not because he was all that good-looking. He considered himself average in that department, but in his circle of peers, young ladies wanted power and money, and they all thought he could provide a lavish lifestyle similar to the rich and famous.

When his father had cut him off financially right after college, he'd been concerned he wouldn't make it. He had a thirst for his father's expensive tastes but didn't have the bank account to go with it. However, Xavier had quickly learned how make it on a lot less and enjoy every minute of it.

He intended to pay his father back every penny he used on this personal sting operation the second the publisher cut him the first check on this next book.

Only, he had to get the damn proposal to them in a couple of months, and he needed to bring down Nightshade and Carlucci in order to even have a true crime book.

"When do you take your LSATs?"

"June, which gives me time to take them again if I don't do well before applying for the following year."

Her heel rested on his thigh, and it proved impossible to keep his hand off her soft skin as he massaged the top of her foot gently. "That means you're a year and a half from entering law school."

"It will be worth it in the long run," she said, the pencil still pressed between her lips.

"What about money between the time our year is up with men and law school?" He hoped his questions appeared to be normal everyday conversation and not probing, investigative inquiry.

"Maybe you'll renew our agreement, and technically I'll still be employed," she said with a forced smile. Her forehead crinkled, and the slight laugh that fell from her lips had a nervous tremble.

She didn't want to renew anything. The question was: Why?

"Maybe I will," he said, running his finger across her arch, watching her toes curl. He could think of another way to make her feet flex and point, but he did his best to squelch that thought. Sex was not on the table, no matter how much he found himself attracted to her. She was the story. The only purpose to flirting had been to find an opening into getting her to talk about why she'd opted for this line of work. "Did you look at all the dresses I had sent over for you to consider for our debut date in public?"

"They are all so gorgeous. I can't decide which one." She set her study material on the coffee table, pulling her knees to her chest, leaving his lap as cold as the winter wind slamming into the windows.

"You can keep the ones you like that fit. We have a few things to attend over the next couple of weekends."

"I can't keep them all. You left the price tag on them and—"

"It's all part of the arrangement." He'd begun to resent Nightshade and everything they represented. If he hadn't picked Cali, some other man would have, and he'd have his dirty hands all over her by now, and that just pissed him off.

"Thank you." She rested her chin on her knee. "I noticed a jewelry box was delivered with the dresses."

"Those, unfortunately, are on loan. Sorry about that." Yeah, on loan from his mother and sisters. His father had put a limit on what he could spend, as well as a two percent interest rate on whatever the total for the year came out to be.

"That's impressive," she said, her lips neither drawn into a smile, nor a frown. "I've always been fascinated by borrowed jewelry."

"It's rented, so to speak. I don't have enough clout to have a designer lend pieces out without a deposit."

"I'll make sure nothing happens to whatever pieces I wear."

"Can I ask you question?" It was now or never.

"Of course."

"Is this your first placement?" he asked.

She nodded.

"How did you end up working for Nightshade?" He studied her facial expressions as she shifted in her seat, closing her arms.

"Easy money to pay for law school." The words tumbled out of her mouth like spilled milk splashing against the tile floor.

"There are lots of ways to pay for college. It seems extreme to take a year or so off." He bit his tongue on asking question after question. He'd have to phrase everything as a statement in a conversation between friends; otherwise, he was going to scare her off.

Her eyes narrowed. "You grew up in a world where everyone got a car for their sixteenth birthday. In my world, if we wanted a car, we had to get a job and pay for it ourselves, and it wouldn't be some shiny new Range Rover, or whatever is under the tarp in the garage."

"I'll give you that. But when I graduated college, I sat in my father's office at home and watched him cut up all my credit cards that he paid. Then he depleted all my bank accounts. All I got to keep was the money I got as a gift and my car, which I sold to buy something I could afford on my own salary."

She tossed her head back and laughed. "Seriously? You think that story makes me believe you understand anything about having to struggle every day? I watched my parents work eighty-hour weeks to stay above water. They wanted to pay for my college but couldn't afford it. The only reason I was able to attend was because I got a partial scholarship. And even now, I'm still paying off my student loans. I bet when you bought that car you could afford, it was paid for with the money you got from selling the car your daddy bought you." Both her eyebrows shot up, daring him to deny it.

He cringed.

"Thought so," she said with a huff.

"I'm sorry, Cali. I didn't mean to insult you. I was just trying to understand why someone like you would go to work for Nightshade."

She opened her mouth, but he shushed her with his finger. "I know this is going to come out ass-backward, but just listen. You're not what I expected."

She batted his hand away. "What did you expect, exactly?"

This might get him slapped. "Certainly not someone who was smarter than me. To be totally honest." Right. As if he'd lay his cards on the table now. "All I wanted was someone to take to functions. I hadn't planned on spending any time with you outside of that."

"Then why the living arrangements?"

Here comes the biggest lie of all. "To get my mother off my back. She's constantly trying to fix me up, wanting me to settle down and get married."

"And what do you plan on telling your mother when our year is up?"

"That I was such a bastard, you had to leave me," he said with his best wicked smile. This conversation was far from over, but he'd give it a break for now.

"That will break her heart." Cali set her feet on the floor. "It's getting late. I should probably go get ready."

"I can't imagine what you'd need to do other than put on a dress, which wouldn't be anywhere near as stunning as you."

"Flattery won't get you places."

"Places? What kind of places?" Her took her by the hand, helping her from the sofa, and drawing her to his chest. His heart hammered in his throat. Touching her had been his first mistake.

This was going to be his second.

Her hands rested on his shoulders. She tilted her head, her tongue peeking out as it glided across her plump, rosy lips. "What are you doing?" she whispered.

"Something that I've been thinking about ever since I saw you at the train station," he mused, drifting his hands over her firm biceps, slowly making their way to her exposed neck. "Feel free to stop me."

Her hot breath tickled his skin as she breathed, sending his body all sorts of signals, and he reacted in such a way that told him he wouldn't last another evening without finding out if the attraction between them was part of the illusion, or something else.

It reminded him of one journalism professor he'd had that had told him, never, under any circumstances, get close to anyone remotely related to your story. No informants. No sources. And certainly not those who could potentially be the center of your piece, and Cali was indeed part of the story.

"This isn't part of the agreement." She bit down on her lower lip.

He blinked. "No. It's not. But that doesn't change the fact that I've been dying to kiss you." Cupping the back of her neck, he melded his mouth against hers, tasting her strawberry and Nutella snack. He kept things slow and controlled, which just made the ache he'd developed over her stronger and more intense. It had started deep in his gut and spread like syrup, filling all the nooks and crannies of a waffle. He'd had almost no experience with relationships, and the few he did have, didn't end well. Women wanted something he couldn't give.

His father's money.

And even if he could, that isn't how he wanted to live his life. Well, except maybe a house like this on the ocean where he could write and do his research. The last two weeks, besides the distraction of the woman in his arms, he'd accomplished more than normal, and he blamed it on the ocean and the view.

His mother constantly told him that no amount of money would make him happy. That money, while a driving force in his father's life, wasn't what drove his father. It wasn't his passion, like his family had been, and Xavier appreciated that.

He deepened the kiss, swirling his tongue around hers, sucking it into his mouth, feeling her full breasts pressed into his body, her tight nipples constricting against his hard chest. He'd dreamt of this moment every night for the last two weeks, and the reality, thus far, surpassed his fantasies with flying colors.

"I should go get ready if we're leaving in an hour."

"I need a cold shower if you're going to leave me hanging."

She patted his chest, turning on her heels. "Cold showers are good for the soul."

Kissing him in his family room had been a momentary lapse in judgment.

Making out with him in the back of the limo on the way to a news award show in the city like a horny teenager on prom night went beyond a bad decision, but it didn't stop her from letting him feel her up.

With his hand on her breast and his thumb dipping inside her strapless dress, caressing her bare nipple, he nibbled on her neck while she ran her hands over his taut shoulders. His tongue felt like velvet inside her mouth. She could kiss him for hours and not get bored for a single second.

"You're irresistible," he murmured against her earlobe.

"Keep talking." She sucked in a deep breath, tugging her dress closer to her body, trapping his finger against her skin.

"Beautiful." His kisses dribbled down her chest, dangerously close to her puckered nipple. "Sexy. Sweet. Dangerous."

"Dangerous, how?"

"I was physically attracted right away, but that I could have managed had it not been for the fact you, the woman, intrigues me on so many levels. You stimulate me intellectually as well as sexually. It's a risky combination."

She wished she didn't understand exactly what he'd meant. After the first night at his house, she'd begun to think he not only didn't find her attractive, but he didn't like her since it felt like he wanted nothing to do with her. She worried that there would be no way he'd lavish her with gifts to sell or cash to help pay off the devil.

Now she had a closet full of designer clothes, and she hoped she'd be able to sneak some out soon. That would be the easy part. The hard part would be not falling for this man. She needed to pull away and not just physically, but emotionally, though she doubted she'd be able to hold out from having sex with Xavier for an entire year, so she needed to build a protective wall around her heart.

He thought she was dangerous? He was a roller coaster about to derail in the middle of an upside-down loop.

"I think we're here," he whispered.

"You've messed up my hair." He'd done more than mess up her hair, but that had been the first thing that came to mind.

"And your boob is hanging out."

She glanced down, hiking up her dress, her cheeks heated. "Wonderful. I think I'll stay in the limo."

He cupped her chin, his green eyes piercing her soul. Protecting herself would be harder than she thought, but she'd have to find a way.

She needed him to not want to renew their agreement after the first year. If she didn't have enough money by then, there was no point anyway.

"Just think of what we can do on the way back."

"We're not having sex for the first time in a car."

He smiled. "At least I know sex is on the table."

"I'm not going to do it on the table." The limo door swung open, and she took the hand of the attendant in front of the Marriott Hotel where the ceremony was being held.

She adjusted her dress just as that reporter, Marlin, snapped his camera, lights flickering in front of her, causing her to lose her balance.

"Back off, Jeff," Xavier said as he stepped in front of her.

The reporter continued taking pictures while asking questions about Cali, which Xavier didn't answer. "Ready?" Xavier pressed his hand at the small of her back, just at the triangular opening of her dress, his fingers dancing over skin as they moved quickly into the hotel lobby, leaving the cold New York winter chill outside.

"If that guy spent more time on real stories, maybe he'd have a bigger following," she said, pausing mid-step as they passed the front desk.

Thompson leaned against the wall, talking with a man she didn't recognize.

"Well, I am up for an award, so maybe a little coverage, even if from that idiot, would be nice."

"You didn't tell me that," she said, keeping her gaze on Xavier and his dashing smile. She passed Thompson without making eye contact, but his presence sent goosebumps across her skin.

"It's for a ten-minute piece I did on the show about crime families in the city."

She coughed, glancing over her shoulder, wondering what the hell Thompson was doing at the Marriott. Especially on a night someone was being honored for exposing things about the very organization Thompson worked for.

"Do you know those men?"

"I don't think so, why?" She swallowed, trying to calm her insides from rattling the floor she walked on. The last thing she needed was Xavier to be suspicious of anything.

"You were very relaxed in the limo, but now you're a bottle of nerves."

"I'm a fish out of water. Of course I'm going to anxious."

"Good point," he said.

She sucked in a deep breath. She was going to need a stiff drink to get through this night.

3

ne week later…

The only way Xavier thought he'd be able to get Cali out of his mind had been to take a business trip. After the awards ceremony, he sent her back in the limo, telling her something came up, and he had to cover a story. It wasn't a total lie, but he didn't trust himself around her, and after seeing her reaction to Thompson, going to bed with her seemed wrong.

No matter how much he wanted it.

He'd spent almost five days hiding out in the city, researching Thompson and finding a few things he didn't like.

Specifically, more images of him and Cali together, so she'd lied about knowing him.

Both pictures had been taken at the family restaurant. One was of her and her parents with Thompson and a man named Lewis Valle who also worked for the

Carluccis in their legal department. That sparked a different kind of interest in Cali's choice of careers and how she planned on using her degree as a criminal lawyer.

Or how the Carluccis planned on using her expertise.

One past employee of Nightshade, who had been terminated after the respective client had decided they weren't compatible, had been Valle's niece, who also had ties to the Carlucci family. Xavier had stumbled onto that information, but the ex-employee was nowhere to be found, and the client was in a relationship, which Xavier suspected had been arranged by Nightshade.

It all came back to what the hell was a mob family using a dating service for? Most likely it had been to launder money, but Xavier didn't think that was the only reason.

Inserting the key into the house in Montauk, he stepped into the foyer. "Cali?" he called.

"In the kitchen." Her voice floated across the room like hot fudge dripping off a spoon, all sweet and gooey.

He inhaled, catching the thick scent of meat sizzling under the broiler. "Smells great in here." He set his backpack on the breakfast bar.

"You said you'd be home at six, so I thought I'd cook you dinner." She pointed to a carafe of red wine. "I hope you don't mind, I've been helping myself."

"Of course not. Did I leave you enough money while I was gone?"

"Plenty," she said with a smile as wide as the sun.

"I hope you used my car to get out of the house. The weather was unseasonably warm this last week."

"I went to visit my parents for a day. Hope that was okay."

"Of course," he said with a frown. "We have an

agreement for companionship, not for me to hold you hostage."

"I didn't mean to imply that you were." She raised her glass, her rosy lips curling over the edge as the wine flowed into her mouth like the soft movement of the river on a still day. "But the people at Nightshade made it clear that we are to always make sure we are within the agreement, so for anything else, we need to ask. You weren't here to ask."

"I'm sorry I was gone so long, but I don't want you to feel like you can't make yourself at home." He stepped around the counter, taking the glass from her hand, inhaling both her fresh, ocean-breeze scent mixed with the full-bodied cabernet. Staring deep into her ocean colored eyes, they held him captive in a world he had no idea existed. It was if she'd cast a spell on him, and he couldn't turn away even if he wanted to.

Setting the glass on the counter, he tipped her chin with his thumb. "I missed you."

"Really?"

He nodded, pressing his thumb over her lower lip. "I'm sorry I had to send you home alone. I was really looking forward to that limo ride." Looping his free arm around her waist, he heaved her to his chest, pressing his knee between her legs. His thigh took the brunt of her heat, and it blinded him with lust.

"I thought about you every morning when I woke up and every night before I went to bed." His body demanded her naked skin. His mind wanted to understand her dealings with a mob family. His heart wanted to turn his brain off and open up to something new and exciting. Something that went beyond companionship and waffled on true love.

He decided for this moment in time, his body would win, closing off the rest. They were two grown-ups who'd entered into an agreement knowing that sex, if they were indeed compatible, would most likely be part of the equation. If he wasn't using her for a story, that would ease his conscience.

But it didn't stop him from tracing a finger from her cute chin, down her soft neck, to the top button of her blouse.

"Your text messages made that clear," she whispered, licking her lips.

Quickly, he unfastened the first three buttons, her chest heaving with every choppy breath she took. Her areola peeked out of the top of her bra. He traced a finger over the top, his muscles tightening as goosebumps lined her skin. The heat in the kitchen no longer belonged to the food in the oven, but the woman in his arms.

"Perfect," he murmured, kneading her breasts until both nipples pushed out of the top of her lacy bra.

Her back arched, raising the tight nubs as he lowered his head, his tongue meeting her flesh, causing an electric pulse.

She moaned as he sucked her into his mouth, his other finger toying, twisting, plucking, and pinching. Her body writhing underneath his, grinding against his thigh, burning him through the fabric of their clothes.

He inched back, making just enough room for him to rip open her jeans and yank them over her hips, cupping her, feeling her wet heat against his palm, his finger finding her hard nub.

"What about dinner?" she said behind a breathy moan.

"I want dessert first." He lifted her, planting her bare ass on the counter as he tossed her jeans and panties across the kitchen. His gaze roamed between his fingers disappearing inside her and her sweet face as she bit down on her lip. Her eyelids lowered over her desire-filled gaze.

She rested her heels on his shoulders, letting her legs fall open, exposing her glistening womanhood. Her hands clasped her breasts, nipples between her forefingers and thumbs, her hips jaunting upward, catching the tip of his tongue, her sweet juices coating him like butter melting in a skillet.

Burying his head between her legs, he licked, kissed, and touched in a frenzy, anxious to make her climax with his mouth. Never before had a woman's orgasm meant so much to him. Not that they didn't, but he could never be satisfied unless she was first.

"Oh…yes…" she ran her hand over his buzzed head, pushing gently and spreading her legs wider.

He dove deeper.

Harder.

Faster.

His tongue circled over her, his teeth nipping. His mouth sucked, while his fingers glided in, twisting and curling inside her, finding that exact spot that made her heels push against him and her hips roll.

Her thighs crashed into his cheeks as her body jerked.

"Xavier," she yelled, moaning and groaning as her body pitched back and forth, shuddering from the purest delight.

He couldn't help but be proud of how she'd reacted to his touch. How she tasted on his tongue. How she continued to roll her hips, demanding more.

Sliding her off the counter, he turned her around, bending her over while he found his wallet, a condom, and kicked his pants to the side.

"Again," she whispered, wiggling against him, her white blouse dangling off her shoulders. "Now." She reached behind her, grabbing his hip with one hand, tugging him forward. "Please. Now."

He groaned as he slowly entered her with one tight stroke, stretching her, watching her lure him deep inside.

"Cali," he said as his eyes rolled to the back of his head, her body clenching over his length, and her hips rocking back into him.

She gripped the counter with one hand, while the other reached between them, gliding between his shaft and herself as he dove in and out with controlled motion, though he knew he wouldn't be able to keep the pace deliberate much longer. His resolve was about to snap into a frenzy of blinding passion. He grit his teeth. His muscles tensed, and his toes curled.

Unable to restrain himself any longer, he slammed into her so hard their bodies smacked against the counter.

She groaned.

"Did I hurt you?"

"God, no," she said with a throaty moan. "I'm right on the edge. Take me there."

"I want to see your face when I do this time." He also needed a few minutes to collect himself and maybe make it last a few seconds longer. Turning her, he lifted her off the floor and carried her to the kitchen table where he sat down, letting her straddle him.

She wasted no time taking him, squeezing her insides tight as she swayed back and forth on his lap. With her hands on his shoulders, she arched her back. "Oh... ahh....yes!" She jerked forward, dropping her head to his shoulder as he pumped himself inside her with no control at all.

"Yes, yes, yes," she whispered in his ear, her hot juices coating him like warm suntan oil.

He stretched his legs out, his toes pointing down as he held her hips while he spilled out violently into her body, the chair shaking with their combined climax.

"Jesus," he said, trying to catch his breath, but the air scorched his lungs. He blinked, but nothing in the room came into focus. "You've blinded me."

She laughed into his neck. "I hope it's temporary so maybe we can do this again."

"Me too. On both accounts. I like watching your face when you call out my name."

She relaxed into his body as he ran his hands up and down her back. Mind-blowing sex was one thing, but this had stolen his ability to think, and he'd never want another woman again.

God, she was going to hate him when this was all said and done.

4

he next morning…

Cali slipped from Xavier's bed, putting on a pair of sweats and a long-sleeve shirt as she padded downstairs to start a pot of coffee and to check her bank account since another paycheck should have come through yesterday. She'd taken almost every penny he'd given her when he'd been on his trip and deposited it, only using what was absolutely necessary for the few fresh food items she'd needed.

She'd also returned two of the dresses and five of them she dropped off at a high-end secondhand store near the city, shocked that she could probably get a thousand dollars for each one. Doing a mental calculation, that meant she had sixty-five thousand and nine months to go. What she really wanted to do was pay off Thompson early, giving her time to relax and enjoy Xavier's company, and hopefully enough time and space so that he'd never find out what she'd done. She'd walk away and never look back.

She told herself it would be easy. He wanted companionship, nothing more, nothing less.

That made her a high-priced hooker.

The sound of footsteps bouncing off the stairs lulled her from the insanity that stirred in her brain. Whatever it took to get her parents out of the grip of the Carluccis would be well worth the shame.

"There you are," Xavier said as he waltzed into the kitchen wearing nothing but flannel pajama bottoms with snowflakes. His defined muscles flexed as he curled his arm around her middle, giving her a quick, but deep kiss. "Want some eggs or something?"

"If you're making them," she said, pushing down the lid to the Keurig. "Over easy with toast and bacon."

He laughed as he pulled out the eggs from the fridge. "Any other specifications?"

"Pinch of salt and a dash of pepper. And I like my bacon crispy." She slipped behind the breakfast bar, flipping open her laptop.

"Good, I tend to burn bacon."

Satisfied with the money in her bank account, she opened one of her study guides on tort law, an area she felt like she knew well but still needed to study.

"What are you doing on that thing?"

She flipped the screen around. "Studying. I suck at taking these kinds of tests, and since I took a couple years off, I need to put that time to good use and make sure I hit it out of the park."

"I'm sure you'll do fine."

She stared at his naked back. "Easy for to say. You don't have to take the test."

"Can I ask why criminal law?" he asked as he tossed some bacon on a cookie sheet and slid it in the oven.

"I'm fascinated with the darker side of human nature

and motivations of people. Why they will commit one crime, but not another."

"Do you want to defend the criminals? Or put them away?"

"Good question. I haven't decided yet." A year ago, she would have said defend. Everyone has the right to a fair trial. No one should be denied counsel, so she'd even consider being a public defender. "I think our criminal system doesn't help those first-time offenders who are dirt poor, who just need a break. Instead, we give them probation, or put them in jail after a plea bargain, and set them up to fail."

"I'll agree with that. I did a story on two kids who were charged with the same crime. One was white, from a privileged background, whose parents hired him a good lawyer. The other couldn't afford one."

"I know where you are going with that, and I'm sure the white kid got off, no record, and the black kid didn't and struggled for the rest of his life."

"Not really. The white kid turned out to be a cold-blooded killer. Murdered his girlfriend and their three-month-old infant."

"That's fucked up," she said, lowering the top of her computer.

"You're right in the sense that he got a slap on the wrist, but he got five of them, and with each arrest, his parents managed to buy him out of trouble. The black man I speak of ended up in jail three times for petty crimes. He works now as a mechanic, trying to make ends meet, bitter over the way the system treated him. Oddly enough, he was arrested the first time at the same party as the white kid. Only, the white boy was arrested for vandalism, and the black kid for stealing jewelry he says he intended to pawn off to help his parents with rent."

"Wait." She held up her finger. "You're talking about Clyde Raymond and Jasper Kirkpatrick. I saw…well, shit. That was your story."

"It was my very first story when I joined Crime Coast Investigations. I did the grunt work but didn't get to report it."

"That was a fascinating case study and not just from a socio-economic position. The assumptions made about Jasper and the fact that his crimes were seen as normal teenage boy issues when in reality, he was a psychopath."

The smell of bacon filled the room as the eggs sizzled in the pan. Xavier waved the spatula. "Clyde was seen as a boy who would become a career criminal when all three times he was stealing, according to him, to help his family. Not that that is an excuse or anything, but his punishments were always stiffer than his rich, white counterpart."

"Who did become a career criminal but got away with it until he killed someone," she added.

"Would you defend someone like Jasper if you were a criminal attorney?" he asked, pushing a plate of steaming hot food across the counter.

She tucked her hair behind her ears, holding the fork in her hand, contemplating her answer. "He deserves good counsel."

"But does he deserve to get off because he had a lawyer who knew how to work the system?" Xavier held up a piece of perfectly cooked bacon, running it across her mouth.

She curled her lips over the tantalizing strip, chomping it between her teeth. "It's an interesting question, but you're innocent until proven guilty, and the emphasis is on proven. That is unless you confess, but we both know a confession can be tossed out as evidence, especially if it appears to be coerced."

"You still haven't answered if you would defend Jasper." He stabbed his eggs with a fork and shoved them into his mouth.

"If I were that kind of an attorney, I would take the case and give him the best counsel possible, but I would also recommend he did whatever it took to stay out of court, and that was his mistake and why he's sitting on death row."

"So, you would have just tried for life without parole."

"If the D.A. offered it, yeah," she said, the eggs melting into her taste buds. She could get used to Xavier's cooking.

She could get used to a lot of things when it came to him.

"If you were the D.A., what would you consider for a plea?"

She laughed. "That's an entirely different question. But I wouldn't take anything less than life plus fifty years and no hope of parole; otherwise, I'd be taking that sucker to court, knowing I'd get the death penalty."

"What about a high-price defense attorney, say for the mafia? Would you consider them for clientele?"

She choked on her last bite of eggs. Last week, she'd worried Xavier sensed her anxiety over being around Thompson and his colleagues at the Marriott in the city. That anxiety had disappeared like the snow melting.

Now it was back ten-fold.

She swallowed. It was just the topic that was making her damned uncomfortable. "If I were to be a defense attorney outside of the public sector, I could choose my clientele, so it would depend on the case." She pushed her plate aside. The butterflies in her stomach fluttered up to her throat. "Again, everyone accused of a crime has a right to counsel, and it would be my job to give them the best defense possible."

"I guess there is no other way to answer that." He leaned across the counter. "We've been invited to a party in the city tonight. I figure we can stay at my loft through the next week. Maybe go see a show and then attend the fundraiser my mother is heading up. She's dying to meet you and has been sending me text messages day and night."

"Not sure I'm ready to meet her. At least around here, when I go out, people just wave and whisper, 'that's the chick Xavier brought home, but no one knows how they met.'"

He took her hands in his, rubbing his thumbs over her skin. "How would you like people to think we met?"

"Anywhere but a dating app," she said with a nervous smile. "What did you tell your parents?"

His lips parted as if surprised by the question. "I've been avoiding telling my parents anything about us, saying its new and I don't know where it's headed."

"And they are okay with that response? Considering it's already been reported that we're living together."

"Yeah. I hadn't thought about that part." He laughed. "I guess we need a cover story. Where do you live?"

"My apartment is near Columbia University."

"I know the area well," he said, nodding. "Ever go to the coffee shop near 114th and Riverside?"

"Eddie's," she said, nodding her head. "They make the best banana muffins."

"I'm partial to the lemon poppy seed ones."

"Oh, those are good too," she said.

"Well, let's say we met there a few months ago. Continued to bump into each other and then exchanged numbers, and things took off from there."

"I really do go there all the time," she said, concern

edging into her brain. "I stopped there when I was home to get some of my things while you were gone."

"I have a friend that lives near there, and we'd often snag a cup of coffee there. So, we met once when I was visiting Charlie and then I just kept showing up, trying to get your number." Xavier winked. "I can persistent."

"I bet you can be." That was an easy enough tale, one even her parents would buy. "Can we add a twist to that story?"

"Is it a kinky twist?"

"Get your mind out of the gutter," she said, shaking her head, though she could think of a few things she'd like to try, especially after last night's marathon between the kitchen, the bed, and finally the shower. "When I signed the agreement, I had to give my parents a reason why I came out here, and I told them you hired me to help with legal research for your latest work."

"So, when you wouldn't go out with me, I hired you and the rest is history. That also explains you sort of bunking with me." He arched a brow, but his smile never faded. "You know, hiring you isn't a bad idea. I'm working on a mafia piece, specifically the Carluccis. Interested?"

Hell, no. What the fuck had she been thinking? Bad move on her part to say anything to him about her parents. She would make sure they never met. And telling her parents she was working for Xavier and his family, she should have come up with a different lie.

Now she was stuck.

"I don't know much about the mafia, so I'm not sure how I could help," she said, backpedaling.

"Oh, come on. You're smart. You understand research and more importantly, you can help me with the legal aspect of my piece. Not just how it relates to the mafia but protecting myself from crossing certain lines." His excitement almost made her forget the same mafia held her parents' business hostage.

Almost.

"What do you say? I'll pay you an assistant salary. I figure this project will last a few months, so does seven grand a month sound fair? It won't be a lot of work, and if we go over a certain—"

"You want to pay me more money?" She held up her hand. Any amount of money would help, and she wasn't about to negotiate when she planned on accidentally losing the one piece of jewelry he'd bought her so she could pawn it.

"I don't want to take advantage of you. If you're going to do the work, you deserve to get paid."

She swallowed her pride. "That's more than fair."

"Wonderful. We'll start on Monday. The limo will be here in two hours to take us into the city. I think that gives us enough time to have a little more fun in the tub."

"I'm game, but it's still a no to doing it in the limo."

"We'll see about that."

When he found out the truth, he'd probably hire the mafia to hide her body.

5

$\mathcal{T}$he city lights beamed through the glass windows on the top of one of the most expensive buildings in the Upper East Side. Xavier's childhood friend, Max, stood next to him, staring out the window, twirling the ice in his nearly empty glass of scotch. "I can't believe you've got yourself a girlfriend."

"I can't believe you're married."

Max laughed. "Amazing any woman would have me, right?"

Xavier sipped his wine, glancing across the room. "Are you sure your wife is alright with this?"

Sadie was one badass federal agent who'd recently been promoted to the organized crime unit and currently worked on a team investigating one of the bigwigs in the Carlucci crime family.

"Honestly, not really and not because she's worried about her job or anything, but because she thinks you're being a dick."

Xavier laughed, though it was forced and didn't stop

the large lump in his throat from expanding. "She's right about that one."

"Why do you think she's involved with the Carluccis?"

Xavier caught Cali's gaze. She smiled sweetly, raising her wine glass to her lips. Every time he stole a glance, she took his breath away.

"After we started dating." Total lie, but even if Max could tell, he wouldn't call Xavier out on it. Not yet anyway. "I found out her parents have a business loan with them."

"Fuck, that can't be good," Max said.

"The question is, did they know what they were getting into when they took it, or was it a shakedown of some kind?"

"I wouldn't be surprised if it were the latter. Sadie can't talk much about it, but she's been unusually busy with work lately and some complaints about one specific person within the organization."

"I hope she's not involved with them. I kind of like this one," Xavier admitted, only kind of was an understatement.

"I'm sure she's not. Hell, she's planning on going to law school. That's got to be a good sign, right?"

Wishful thinking. The mafia had their own legal team, and they were some of the brightest attorneys in the business.

"Here she comes," Xavier said.

"I'll go get Sadie."

Xavier stared over his wine glass at the vision waltzing across the floor. Life certainly knew how to hand him a twist of fate. He had no idea what to expect when he'd become a client of Nightshade other than combing through a dozen or so women, looking for just one with a connection to the Carluccis.

He found her.

But he'd lost his heart a little too fast.

"Your friends are very nice for insanely rich folk."

"Most of them, anyway." He wrapped a protective arm around her waist. "I bet you got hit on at least three times since I left your side."

She shook her head. "You made it very clear when you introduced me to people that I was off limits."

"Glad my idiot fiends listened."

"Me too." Palming his cheek, she kissed him, her tongue easing between his lips. "Are we taking a limo back to the loft?"

He groaned, squeezing her hips. "Damn straight we are."

"You're intoxicating," she whispered against his ear, her hot breath rolling off his skin. "I keep doing unexpected things with you."

"Is that good or bad?"

"I haven't decided yet."

"Get a room," Max's voice boomed across the apartment, startling Xavier.

He pulled Cali closer, not wanting to let her go, wishing he'd never asked his buddy to have his wife bring up the Carlucci name. He wanted to go back in time to a point where he could find a way to meet her on his own, be ignorant about her knowledge of the mafia, and where he didn't have to ask probing questions intended to out her mob connections.

He just wanted to get to know the woman in his arms.

"Ah, new love," Sadie said, her hand tucked into Max's elbow. She might have come from money, but she had more refinement than most people. But she had a razor-sharp tongue too. "Remember when we were like that?"

"Are you kidding? We're still like that; we just have

enough class to keep it private." Max kissed his wife's cheek. "Cali, meet my wife, Sadie, the best woman in the world, and the greatest FBI agent specializing in organized crime you'll ever meet."

"Ignore my husband. He's had one too many."

Xavier held his breath, feeling every muscle in Cali's body tense.

Definitely not a good sign.

"My wife is being modest. She's an expert on the Carluccis, and Xavier is interviewing her for a piece he's working on."

"You really need to learn to zip it," Sadie said, patting Max's chest. "I don't think Xavier's girlfriend wants to hear about the Carluccis."

"I don't know about that," Xavier said, setting the trap. "She's helping me with my research now."

"Really," Sadie said with a little too much inflection. "Find anything interesting about the Carluccis?"

"I haven't started working on it yet, and I don't really know much about that family, specifically." Cali leaned away from Xavier.

He took that as a big fat negative sign.

"I will say I'm fascinated by the mafia mentality and how that has changed over the years," Cali said, keeping her distance.

Xavier wasn't sure what to think about that. She willingly continued the conversation after being visibly uncomfortable. He needed to understand why she backed away and if it was because she was one of them.

Or being extorted by them.

Both equally plausible.

"Changed how?" Sadie asked. "In my line of work, the only change I've seen is that we're more focus on gang-related crimes than the mob."

Xavier should offer to refill drinks, letting Sadie do her own brand of investigative questions, making her own judgment about Cali and her potential ties to the mafia. But his overprotective instincts kicked in.

Or maybe it was his desire to pretend he wasn't in the middle of a story that he'd put his entire career and family life on hold for.

"Organized crime has become more white-collar in nature," Cali said, her hands folded across her chest in a closed off, defensive stance. "The gang dynamic has taken over where the mob used to rule the streets."

"You're right about that," Sadie said. "But that doesn't change the way the mob handles things that go wrong within their own organization. Just a month ago, we pulled a man from the Hudson. Murdered. He was connected to the Carluccis and was a member of their exclusive men's club, Nightshade."

Xavier coughed, nearly spitting out his wine.

"Doesn't mean he was killed by them," Cali said, her words laced with conviction. "I've never heard of Nightshade."

He'd never survive the next few months if she were in cahoots with the mob.

"It appears to be a legit club, but I highly doubt it," Sadie said. "And I've seen a lot of violent crimes when it comes to the mafia."

"I don't know about any of that." Cali chomped down on her fingernail. "But I look forward to finding out more."

He hoped so, but right now he had his doubts, and he contemplated sending her back to the loft alone in the limo.

He wouldn't be able to resist her charm.

---

6

*C*ali didn't know what was worse: the fact she'd taken the necklace and hid it in her purse, waiting for Xavier to notice it wasn't on her neck or that she was willing to use sex to deflect any real conversation.

She hiked her dress over her hips, exposing her tiny thong. Her hands palmed his face while her tongue went on a mission to taste every crevice in his mouth. His fingers dug into bare flesh, slowing her desperate movements.

The limo driver navigated the city streets, turning randomly as Xavier told him to go anywhere. To drive until he was told to take them home.

She didn't even care that the driver knew they were having sex in the back seat. She figured it happened enough times that the knowledge no longer affected the driver.

Kissing her way down Xavier's chest as she unfastened each button, she tried to push the events of the evening from her mind.

Except one thing stuck out.

Sadie, the FBI agent, said that the Feds were actively

investigating unethical business practices of certain businesses owned and operated by the Carluccis. The current contract her parents had signed with Thompson and his loan company made him a partner. God only knew what he might be running through the restaurant.

And then there was the mention of Nightshade. If the FBI were investigating that, then Xavier would be too.

If he wasn't already.

"Cali," Xavier whispered, gently lifting her off his lap, smoothing her dress down over her thighs. "I'd like nothing more than to bury myself inside you, but your mind is somewhere else right now."

"What are you talking about?" She reached for him, but he curled his fingers around her wrists, resting their hands on his thighs.

"You tell me," he said, his tone neither accusatory nor angry, but it had a certain edge that made her squirm.

"I'm right here with you."

He traced a path up her arm with his finger, tickling her skin. "When we're together, I want you to be only thinking about your personal pleasure, or mine. Just now, I could tell your mind was on something else; it wasn't anything related to taking me in that hot mouth of yours."

"I have only one thing on my mind." Slowly, she unbuttoned his slacks and lowered the zipper, pressing her palm over him.

"Cali, stop." Xavier shifted, pushing her away.

She bit back a sob. She'd been rejected before, but never by a man who was paying her.

Worse, she was falling so hard for him, it knocked her senseless because it had only been in this moment that she knew without a doubt, she loved Xavier.

And she was going to betray him.

And he was going to destroy her the second a story about the mob came out.

Closing her eyes tight, she held back the tears that threatened to expose her for what she really was.

"Look at me," he commanded.

She snapped her gaze in his direction. "Why are you being like this? You're the one who wanted to have sex in the limo."

"You've lied to me," he whispered so softly she wondered if she'd heard him correctly.

"What are you talking about." A single tear rolled down her cheek.

"You tell me."

"There is nothing to tell." She folded her arms across her chest, scooting to the other side of the seat. She needed to be as far away from him as possible.

"Your necklace, it's missing," he said, pointing at her cleavage.

She glanced down, sucking in a deep breath, trying to hide her shame. "Oh, no." She clutched her fist against her chest. "It must have fallen off. Maybe it's in the limo." She glided her fingers in the seats and looked on the floor, lifting the floor mats. Her heart hammered against her chest so fast she thought she might pass out. "It has to be here somewhere," she managed, knowing the exact location of the piece of jewelry.

"I hope you didn't lose it at the party."

"Maybe we should call your friends. Ask them to look for it."

The limo driver's voice came over the speaker, letting them know he was about to pull up in front of Xavier's building.

He stepped from the vehicle with a tight jaw. He didn't

even take her hand or touch the small of her back as they waited for the elevator.

Once inside the spacious, top-floor loft apartment, Xavier took her purse from her hands.

"I have some makeup in there I want to put away," she said, mortified as he flipped it open, pulling out her wallet. "What are you doing?"

"I have a couple of questions for you." He pulled out the receipt the woman at the secondhand store had given her for the dresses. Reaching in her purse once again, he held up the necklace. "I could almost understand selling the dresses, considering I know you don't have a lot of money and are saving for law school, but what I don't get is why would you lie about losing this? Did you plan on selling it too?"

Fuck. Fuck. Fuck.

Think. Think. Think.

But her mind went blank. Not even a bad lie popped into her brain.

"You wouldn't understand," she muttered, collapsing onto the sofa, covering her eyes with her forearm.

"Try me," he said.

She heard his feet shuffle across the room, but she didn't bother to glance up to find out where he went. Didn't matter.

"And while you're at it, explain to me how you know Thompson."

She laughed. A horrible response, but it was more of a sarcastic laugh anyway. "Does it matter?"

"Yeah. Actually it does." His tone had turned cold and harsh. The lights from the other buildings shone through the glass windows like a kaleidoscope, framing his body with an array of colors.

"Why? You already believe certain things about me,

and I'm getting the feeling that you've been deceitful as well."

"I have. I'm willing to tell you the truth, but you've got to be honest with me first."

Why the fuck not? Things couldn't get any worse. "I need two hundred and fifty thousand dollars to pay off Thompson." She sat up, smoothing down her dress, and stared at Xavier, who stood in front of the coffee table with his hands on his hips, glaring as if she needed a good scolding.

"Pay him off for what?" Xavier asked.

"He took advantage of my parents, getting them to sign a legal, but questionable contract ethically, and now if I don't get him the money, they will force my parents to turn over their restaurant."

"A legal shakedown, go figure," he said, shaking his head. "How much do you have to date?"

"About sixty-five thousand."

"Is that every penny you have?"

"Yes," she admitted, letting out a sigh of relief. While she knew she'd lost Xavier for good, it felt good to unburden herself.

"So, this wasn't about saving for law school at all, was it."

"Obviously not." She waved her hand toward the end of the sofa. "Would you please sit down. You're making me nuts."

"No." His green orbs speckled with blue highlights and filled with hurt. "Do you care about me at all?"

"That's rich, coming from you, because I bet you've been using me for some story."

"Doesn't answer my question," he said behind a tight jaw.

"But you said you'd tell me the truth."

63

"I will. But not just yet. I need to know a few more things first, like how you feel about me."

"Based on the way you're looking at me now, my answer wouldn't matter because you can't stand me." She decided she needed to be on his level, so she stood but put more distance between them by standing behind the sofa. Was probably good to put a large object in the way.

"I'm pissed at you, but that doesn't change the fact that I've managed to let myself fall madly in love with you." There was no denying the anger dripping from his words, but a trickle of devotion intertwined in his tone.

"Love me? Are you crazy?"

"I just might be." He let out a long breath. "Did Thompson force you to become an employee of Nightshade?"

"Forced isn't the correct word. He made an offer I couldn't refuse."

"What about the fine print in that contract?"

"I negotiated slightly different terms and had an addendum drawn up, that they signed. Me and my parents are free once I give them the money. But I have to do it by December 31."

"Oh, Cali. They aren't going to let you go without a fight. Especially when they can terminate my membership at any time. They are going to make sure you never meet that deadline. The Carluccis and their employees can be dangerous people and difficult to deal with."

She cleared her throat, taking a moment to process the information. "What do you mean? You paid dues for a year. How can they just kick you out?"

"The contract I signed says that at any time and without any reason, they can terminate my membership. I didn't care because I hoped to have cracked the story in the first three months…Shit."

"What?"

"They played me too. I wondered why it was so easy for me to join. They wanted me close to see what I'd do and at the sign of trouble, they'd rip up my contract, probably before I had any story."

"What is the story, exactly?" She clenched her fists. "Wait. If it's to expose me as a call girl, I don't want to know."

"Not you, or any of the girls. Look. You're doing what you have to in order to protect your family. I can respect that." He closed the gap, reaching for her hand.

She took a step back.

"Cali. I want to know if I'm going to have to get over you or find a way for us to move past the lies we both told, so we can start fresh."

"What?" She blinked. Her instincts weren't very sharp lately, and he could easily be manipulating her.

But for what purpose at this point?

"I didn't welcome my feelings, but I can't change them. I care very deeply for you, and I want us to explore what we could have."

"Didn't welcome. Now that's what a girl wants to hear." She took a tentative step, resting her hands on his shoulders. "I care about you," she said with a shaky voice. "I didn't want to, because I didn't want to hurt you, but I couldn't stop it."

"I'm going to need to call my dad in the morning. If we don't have enough to expose the Carluccis, then I'll have to rethink how we go forward. I want to make sure you don't have to give Thompson a dime and that your parents get their restaurant."

"We could just continue with the agreement," she said, knowing that there was no way Xavier would go for that.

"I'd rather not. I'm digging myself into a financial hole

as it is, and honestly, I never intended to spend a year with you." He pulled her against his chest. "That last part didn't come out right because I really do want to spend time with you."

"How are you digging yourself into a hole? You're rich." Shit, that made her sound like a gold digger.

"I don't have that kind of money. I have maybe a hundred grand in my savings, but most of it is in stocks and bonds. My dad is the rich dude, and he's kind of hell-bent on not sharing unless we work for the family business, and with me that was never going to happen."

"This loft? The limos? Cars? What is all that then?"

"Everything but the loft my father let me borrow, including the money, which I have to pay back with interest. And that necklace." He pointed to the counter in the kitchen. "That's my little sister's."

She dropped her hands. "I have to know what the story is that you're chasing."

"I want to blow the lid off what the Carluccis are doing. I've talked to a few ex-employees, and it's not good. It doesn't end with one contract. And some of the men that use the club are bad news."

"Why go through Nightshade to dig up your story? It's a legit business, sort of."

"I have a source inside the club. He's been giving me some intel. I've also met with a woman whose face was used for a punching bag."

Cali covered her mouth, stopping a gasp from echoing through the room. "You wanted to expose them as a high-priced hooker service?"

"Not exactly, but that would be a good start."

"That would make me look bad when the story hits," she muttered. "Did you pick me because you knew about my—"

"I became a client of Nightshade because I'm trying to find out how they use the corporation for their operations, and you seemed like the best way to get that information. I didn't know anything about your situation until we met, and I did some digging. At one point, I worried that maybe you actually worked for Carlucci and were a plant to see what story I was working on."

"Well, you were wrong."

He had the audacity to smile. "I was so wrong about that, and I'm sorry." He yanked her to his chest.

She slammed her fist down, trying to push him away, but he held her tighter. "You break this story, you'll out me as an employee, and I'll lose any chance of going to law school."

He shook his head. "You and I are going to expose the Carluccis, together. Remember, you work for me, as my assistant. Besides, you're my girlfriend, and no way will I let one bad word be printed about you."

7

*C*ali got out of the limo and stared at the largest home she'd ever seen up close and personal. "You grew up here?"

"I did," Xavier said, lacing his fingers through hers, but she yanked her hand away.

It wasn't so much that she was still mad over the knowledge he'd been using her from the start. She'd be a hypocrite if that were the case. However, she still held a fair amount of shame over what she'd done, and now his parents would know the truth of her betrayal.

They'd hate her, and that was no way to start a relationship.

There was no way in hell she and Xavier would make it, and the sooner she accepted that, the better they'd both be.

"How long are you going to remain ticked off?" he asked, placing his hand on her back, guiding her up the walkway toward the front door.

"I can tell you're still mad at me too, so..."

He let out a slight laugh. "You're good at deflecting attention. If I ever need a lawyer, I know who I'm calling."

"If I ever make it to law school."

He leaned in, kissing her cheek. "You will, and you'll be a great attorney, and I'll beam with pride at your graduation."

"Anyone ever tell you that you can be corny as hell?"

"Never." He pushed open the door. "Mom? Dad? We're here."

She swallowed, holding her chin high as she stepped into a two-story foyer with a split staircase. It looked more like a room than an entryway with a love seat positioned between the railings and wing-back chairs in the corners.

"Xavier." A woman wearing a pair of dark slacks and a red sweater stretched out her arms as she entered the space.

"Hey, Mom." He kissed her cheek. "This is Cali."

"Nice to meet you. We've heard a lot about you over the last two months."

The butterflies in her gut turned to cement, landing in the center of her stomach. His parents had known from the beginning what Xavier had planned, but her situation was brand-new information, and she had no idea what they thought about her, or her parents.

"It's nice to finally meet you too." She held out her hand, but his mother pushed it aside and pulled her into a warm embrace. "I'm so sorry for what your parents are going through. I can only imagine how difficult it has been."

"Thank you."

His mother had a sweet, caring smile and seemed genuine in her greeting, but that didn't settle Cali's nerves.

"Your father is waiting in his office."

"Max and his wife are about a half hour behind us.

Sadie is bringing her partner. Can you send them back when they get here?" Xavier asked.

His mother nodded.

As they walked through a long hallway, Cali glanced at all the family portraits hanging on the wall. Images of him and his sisters in various activities. A few candid snapshots of the family along with a large family portrait at the end of the hall. "You don't have any brothers."

"Nope. Just four sisters. One older and three younger. But don't mention my older sister, Bonnie. She's become the black sheep, and it upsets both my parents."

"Good to know."

For a woman in love, there was so much she didn't know about Xavier and his life.

She paused mid-step in front of an open door. A man, who looked like an older version of Xavier, sat behind a big, dark desk. He peered over his reading glasses. "Come in," he said with a deep voice. "You must be Cali." He stood, stretching out his hand.

"Yes, sir," she said, trying to swallow the thick lump in her throat. The office was filled with trophies and pictures of Xavier and his sisters. Obviously, Mr. Sumner felt great pride for his family.

"Son," his father said with a nod. "Please sit down."

"Did you read the information I sent?" Xavier asked, cutting to the chase.

His father nodded. "Cali. What do you think? More importantly, what do you want?"

"The only thing I want right now is to make sure my parents get to keep their business and never have to deal with Thompson or the Carluccis again. Long term, I'd like to see all the Carluccis behind bars."

"And you and Xavier? Do you have a long-term—"

"Dad. Seriously? That's none of your business."

His father shrugged. "Hey. I promised your mom I'd ask, and you know how she gets."

"It's a fair question." Cali knew a relationship based on lies and betrayal from both parties was nothing but a recipe for disaster. "I have no idea. My sole focus is on helping my parents and taking down Carlucci."

"Even if it puts you and Xavier in the middle of the story?"

"I'll do anything to save the family business," she said.

"I appreciate your honesty and directness," his father said. "And I admire your dedication to your family. It takes a lot of courage to do what you have."

"I think there is one more item we need to discuss," she said, shifting her gaze to Xavier.

"Sadie," Xavier said, nodding. "I told her everything and gave her all my notes."

"Does she have enough to make an arrest?"

"We're getting close," Xavier admitted.

Xavier reached out and took her hand in his. This time, she didn't pull away. After this was all over, maybe they could start over.

Xavier paced in his father's office while Sadie, her partner, Rex, and Cali went over the plan.

Dumb fucking plan.

"Stop," Cali said, looking over her shoulder as she leaned over the desk. "I can't think with all that stomping around."

"I don't like this at all."

"It's not your call," Cali said.

He was about to protest more, but his phone rang, and

it was one of the businesses in the same hood as her parents. "This is Xavier Sumner."

"This is Rick Wellington. I own Wellington Meats."

"Yes. Mr. Wellington, thank you for getting back to me."

Xavier had called ten businesses. Three of them told him to take a hike before he finished asking about Thompson and his contract and if there was any connection to Nightshade. Two of them flat out denied it. One store, no one answered, but four, including Wellington Meats, took the information, said they hadn't done business with the man, but would look into it. Xavier knew they were lying but figured if he played his cards right, he'd get what he needed.

"I spoke to a couple other business owners. While, I've yet to fall below the threshold, two of them had and both had a daughter who ended up working for Nightshade." The man sniffled. "One of the girls has been missing for six months. She'd just turned twenty when she went to work at the exclusive club. She told her parents she was waiting tables, but that wasn't the truth at all."

"I'm sorry. We'd like to put a stop to this and expose Carlucci."

"There are four business owners willing to help you."

"I'll need you to give me every document you signed, and we'll need access to your bookkeeping."

Sadie glanced in his direction, and he made eye contact. This could be the big break they both looking for.

"Like I said, I'm still above water, but not for long. I signed that contract with Thompson, and when he pulls the plug, I'll be left with nothing."

"Jesus Christ," Xavier said under his breath. "What exactly is the clause in the contract?"

"If my profits fall under a certain percentage, they have the right to take over. But the kicker is, that only happened because I used one of his suppliers, which had bad meat, higher costs, and other issues that forced me to take a huge hit. I knew there was a buyout, but I had no idea it was so low. Everyone I've talked to is in a similar situation. None of us can afford to lose our businesses. In some cases, it's the family's only source of income."

"Can you gather everyone? And is everyone willing to talk with the FBI?"

Cali stood, making her way across the room. She rested her hands on his shoulders, her gaze locked on his.

"Yes. We are. Name the time and place, and we'll be there."

"Meet us at the Banister's place. Two hours. Bring all the legal documentation. We'll have a lawyer there along with the Feds. Trust me, we'll figure this out. Very worst-case scenario, we blow the whistle using my television show to do it."

"Thank you, Mr. Sumner. We all appreciate your efforts."

"It's my pleasure." He tapped his phone, ending the call. "Sadie, set up your sting. We get Thompson singing like a canary, and you'll get the biggest bust of your career so far, and I'll get that show and another book deal." He cupped Cali's chin. "You'll become the best damn lawyer this town has ever seen." He brushed his lips across hers. "And we'll get to find out what this thing is between us without anything hanging over our heads."

8

*C*ali pushed a contract across the table at the diner Xavier picked out. Her father and mother were sitting across from her, with Thompson and his slimy body to her left.

"You can sign this," she told her parents. A copy of it had been given to a legal advisor for the FBI, and it was deemed legal and binding and severed all business ties with her parents and Thompson. Now all she had to do was get her parents to leave and help Sadie make her arrest.

Easy peasy.

Right.

"I'm impressed you were able to get this kind of cash in such a short period of time. What did you do? Sell yourself?"

Her mother gasped.

"I have a rich boyfriend," she said, holding her father's stare. Boy, was he going to have a ton of questions when this was over.

"I noticed you and that Sumner guy at the Marriott. He's some sort of crime reporter, right?" Thompson asked.

Sadie had warned her how quickly this could go sideways if she wasn't careful.

"And a novelist, but now we're splitting hairs." She watched her parents sign on a few different pages.

Her father handed them back, staring at her with the same evil eye he used to give her as a kid when she'd stayed out past curfew.

"Mom, Dad, you can go now," she said.

"Not until I get my money."

"I've got it." She held up an envelope of cash with a shaky hand. "My parents leave, and you get your money."

"Fine," Thompson said. "It's been nice doing business with you."

"Cali," her mother said with wide eyes. "You're coming with us, right?"

"In a minute." The plan had always been to have her parents sign and leave. They'd been coached on what to say and do. Cali needed them to follow through. She understood their concern for her safety, but there were six federal agents armed and ready if this didn't work.

Her dad helped her mom from the booth.

She watched them as they left, constantly glancing over their shoulders. Had to be hard to leave their only child with a man who'd been bullying half the neighborhood.

She moved to the other side of the booth.

Thompson stared at her with an ominous smile. "My money," he said with a snarl.

She placed the large envelope on the table, keeping her hands pressed against the paper. "Along with the cash, there is a key to a locker at the train station. In the locker is the same buyout for every business in this neighborhood." She pushed another envelope across the table. "Here are the contracts, all signed, voiding the previous ones. They just need your John Hancock."

"Are you fucking kidding me?" he leaned back in his seat. "Like hell am I going to do that."

"What you're doing borders on illegal."

He laughed. "No, it doesn't. Not my fault if they don't understand what they are agreeing to."

"You mislead them regarding your buyout clauses, and then you force your bogus suppliers on them. I think, if taken to a court of law, a judge and jury might see things differently. Not to mention forcing young ladies to go to work at Nightshade, which come on, let's call the kettle black, that place isn't companionship for hire."

"You're mistaken, little girl." He leaned forward, keeping his hands under the table. "You talk a good game, but you're way out of your league. The only reason why we're letting your parents off the hook is because you proved to be more resourceful than we expected, and we don't need that boyfriend of yours poking around in our business."

"We?" she asked.

"I have business partners," he responded with narrowed eyes. "And while amused by your creativity, they won't be pushed into backing out of the other binding, legal contracts. You can't muscle me. Besides, you entered Nightshade of your own accord. I only offered you the job. There was no twisting your arm."

"Really? You've got to be kidding, right? I'd say it was two hundred and fifty thousand of twisting." She waved her hand dismissively. "But what I want to know is why does Carlucci really want with these businesses?" Her heart beat so hard that along with the federal agents listening in, she bet the entire diner could hear it.

Thompson cocked his head.

"Who?"

"Don't play dumb. I know you work for them, and I

know it's a legit," she held up her fingers making quotation marks, "business, but the Carluccis have other dealings shadier than this one, and I have to think that whatever those are, it's the reason they want to put these poor people out on the streets and take their daughters and prostitute them out."

"You've got it all figured out, don't ya?"

A hard object hit her leg with a gentle tap. She jerked her knee away.

"That's a gun. In case you were wondering," Thompson said.

"Are you threatening me?" Her throat rattled worse than her hands shaking against the table.

"Consider it a warning. Now, I'll take the money, and the key with all the other cash, but I'm not signing anything, nor will we be negotiating any new contracts. We're taking over those establishments, and there isn't a damn thing any of you can do about it. Nor can you stop us from hiring any woman at Nightshade." He jabbed her thigh, pressing the muzzle of the gun hard against her leg. "If you meddle in my business again, I'll make sure your parents don't make it to their next birthday. Got it?"

She nodded, fighting back the tears. She hoped Sadie had all she needed to make the arrest.

"Watch your back," Thompson said as he rose, stuffing the gun in his pocket. "Mr. Carlucci isn't a man who takes too kindly to people like you."

She kept her hands flattened on the Formica tabletop, gaze glued to Thompson as three agents stormed the diner, guns pointed, yelling at him to hit the deck.

"You're a dead woman," Thompson said as Sadie slapped a set of handcuffs around his wrists. "You and your parents."

The tears broke free, streaming down her cheeks. She dropped her forehead to her hand, letting the sobs bellow from deep in her gut.

"Cali." Xavier's voice filled her brain and engaged her heart with a sense of belonging she never wanted to lose.

His strong arms wrapped around her body like a favorite blanket. "Shhhh, it's going to be all right."

"I've never been so scared in my life." She rested her head on his shoulder.

"You did good," he said, smoothing down her hair. "I'm sorry we had to put you through that."

"I'd do anything for my parents." She glanced up at Xavier. "I owe you a lot of money, and I have no idea how I'm going to pay it back."

"What money? We got the cash you gave to Thompson back."

"Oh. That's right."

His smile brightened the room and filled her heart with joy. He leaned in and kissed her temple.

"Sorry to break up the party, but until we have Carlucci in custody, I need all of you in a safehouse."

"How long will that take?" Xavier asked, keeping her tucked neatly against his chest.

"We've got the warrant for Nightshade, all the local businesses, as well as his home. I'd say twenty-four tops. But I've got to make this stick. We don't want that asshole getting off on a technicality."

"As long as Cali and I get our own room, that's fine."

She slapped him on the shoulders. "Our parents will be there. I don't think—"

"Our parents will get over it." He cupped her face, fanning his thumbs across her cheeks. "Cali, I love you."

"That's not taking things slow."

"Slow is overrated." He cocked his head. "Are you going to seriously leave me hanging like this?"

She smiled. "And to think it only took a good old-fashioned shakedown for me to find the love of my life."

EPILOGUE

 *our years later…*

"California Banister Sumner."

Xavier puffed out his chest. "That's my wife," he whispered to his mother-in-law sitting next to him at the commencement ceremony. They'd only been married for a few months, having had a winter ceremony at his parents' place out on Montauk. Right on the beach. Snow and all.

"Go, Cali!" he yelled as the dean handed her a diploma.

"You're more excited than she is," her father said.

"He's always been hyper," his mother said.

He ignored both sets of parents as he stared at the woman who rocked his world.

She glanced out over the stage and gave him a smile and a little wave.

His leg shook for the next twenty minutes. All he wanted to do was take his bride and twirl her around.

JEN TALTY

She'd worked so hard to be a lawyer, and he couldn't be prouder.

Or happier.

As soon as the commencement ended, he raced through the crowd, weaving left and right like a football player dashing to the goal line until he found Cali.

"My wife. Attorney-at-law." He hugged her, lifting her in the air.

"You left our parents in the dust," she said, laughing.

"Couldn't help myself." He kissed her like a husband would in the privacy of their own home. He didn't care if people stared.

"Stop," she said, pressing her hands against his chest.

"You're spoiling my fun." He tucked a piece of her hair behind her ear, admiring the new diamond earrings he'd gotten her for graduation. She hadn't been one of those wives who demanded jewelry, but diamond earrings she'd been mentioning for a while, so he splurged.

"There will be plenty of time for that when we get home."

"We still haven't christened the one guest room that still doesn't have furniture."

"I was thinking about what I wanted to put in that room," she said.

"It's a bedroom. How hard can that decision be? Just pick a set you like."

"I have something else in mind," she said, palming his cheek, giving it a couple of love taps.

"Like what?"

"Baby furniture."

Thank you for taking the time to read *NIGHTSHADE*. I hope you enjoyed reading it as much as I enjoyed writing

82

it. Please feel free to leave an HONEST review on Amazon and/or Goodreads

Sign up for my Newsletter (https://dl.bookfunnel.com/6atcf7g1be) where I often give away free books before publication.

Join my private Facebook group (https://www.facebook.com/groups/191706547909047/) where she posts exclusive excerpts and discuss all things murder and love!

Never miss a new release. Follow me on Amazon:amazon.com/author/jentalty And on Bookbub: bookbub.com/authors/jen-talty

THE LOST SOLDIER

THE LOST SOUL

Coming soon!

THE LOST CONNECTION

Special Forces Operation Alpha

BURNING DESIRE

BURNING KISS

BURNING SKIES

BURNING LIES

BURNING HEART

BURNING BED

The Brotherhood Protectors

ROUGH JUSTICE

ROUGH AROUND THE EDGES

The Twilight Crossing Series

THE BLIND DATE

SPRING FLING

SUMMER'S GONE

Coming soon!

WINTER WEDDING

Witches and Werewolves

LADY SASS

ALL THAT SASS

Coming soon!

NEON SASS

PAINTING SASS

ABOUT THE AUTHOR

Welcome to my World! I'm an Award-Winning and Bestselling Author of Romantic Suspense, Contemporary Romance, and Paranormal Romance. DARK WATER, book 2 in the NY STATE TROOPER series hit number 10 in Barnes and Nobel overall. THE BLIND DATE hit number 1 in the Contemporary Romance/Kindle Worlds List on Amazon. JANE DOE'S RETURN won both THE MOLLY and the BEACON before being published by the WILD ROSS PRESS.

I first started writing while carting my kids to one hockey rink after the other, averaging 170 games per year between 3 kids in 2 countries and 5 states. My first book, IN TWO WEEKS was originally published in 2007. In 2010 I helped form a publishing company (Cool Gus Publishing) with NY Times Bestselling Author Bob Mayer where I ran the technical side of the business through 2016.

I'm currently enjoying the next phase of my life...the empty NESTER! My husband and I spend our winters in Jupiter, Florida and our summers in Rochester, NY. We have three amazing children who have all gone off to carve out their places in the world, while I continue to craft stories that I hope will make you readers feel good and put a smile on your face.

Visit my website at http://jentalty.com

Sign up for Jen's Newsletter
*(*https://dl.bookfunnel.com/rg8mx9lchy*) where she often gives*
away free books before publication.

Join Jen's private Facebook group
(https://www.facebook.com/groups/191706547909047/) where
she posts exclusive excerpts and discuss all things murder and love!

[O] instagram.com/jen_talty

[a] amazon.com/author/jentalty

[BB] bookbub.com/authors/jen-talty

Printed in Great Britain
by Amazon